MARVEL AVENGERS

PINT-SIZE POWER

AUTUMN
PUBLISHING

Ant-Man and Wasp were having a bad day. Someone had broken into their lab and stolen their growth serum.

"We need to run some DNA samples through the database at Avengers Tower to find out who is behind this crime," said Ant-Man.

At Avengers Tower, Ant-Man soon got his answer. "It's Scarlet Beetle. I wonder what he wants with our growth serum? It could cause a catastrophe in the wrong hands!" he said to the Avengers.

Meanwhile, on the other side of the city, Scarlet Beetle was having an awesome day.

Using the stolen vials of growth serum, he was gathering an army of giant insects in an attempt to conquer the world.

"We need to squash this Scarlet Beetle," said Iron Man. "Shouldn't be too hard. He's only a bug."

"Don't underestimate him," said Wasp. "He may be a bug, but he's—"

"Got it," said Iron Man, cutting her off. "Let's go."

The Avengers were under attack as soon as they arrived.

"Whoaaa!" wailed Iron Man, as he suddenly found himself surrounded by a swarm of gigantic yellow jackets.

"Yellow jackets are part of the wasp family," Wasp informed him.

"Cool fact!" cried Iron Man. "But can you help?"

Wasp smiled, as she stunned the yellow jackets with her Wasp Sting.

Down below on the ground, Hulk, Black Widow, Hawkeye and Thor had their own problems bugging them. They were being overrun by a swarm of giant insects from all sides. And things were about to get even worse.

Suddenly, Scarlet Beetle appeared above the rooftops, riding on the back of a huge bug.

"You can't destroy my army," he cackled. "Insects outnumber humans on this planet. Soon we will rule the world, and there is nothing you can do about it."

"Not today, tiny creature!" shouted Thor, hurling his mighty hammer.

"Nooo!" cried Scarlet Beetle, as he found himself crashing towards the roof.

Hulk smiled as he watched Scarlet Beetle fall. But at the last moment, the mutant pest shot out his claws and managed to pull himself up to safety.

"Ha-ha-ha!" cried Scarlet Beetle. "Now get ready for Act Two."

Suddenly, there was a terrible, piercing screech. The noise made Hulk and Thor grab their heads in agony.

They were in so much pain that they didn't notice the approaching swarm of stick insects.

With an evil cackle, Scarlet Beetle smashed his way through a skylight into the building below.

Suddenly, Ant-Man zoomed past and sprayed the stick insects with a mist. "That sound is coming from the stick bugs," he cried. "They use it to disarm their enemies."

Hulk rubbed his head. "Mist made bugs small."

"It's my new antidote," said Ant-Man. "But I don't have enough to shrink the entire insect army."

"Then we will just have to work as a team to take down these monstrous creations," said Thor. "What are we waiting for?"

Ant-Man nodded, and all the Super Heroes leapt into an epic battle of man versus insect.

"Iron Man, aim for their wings, not their bodies," Wasp commanded. "Their skeletons are on the outside."

"Thor!" Ant-Man shouted. "Stir up some thunder. The vibrations will calm them down." But nobody listened.

"Why won't they listen?" cried Ant-Man.

"They think they're too good for us bugs," replied Wasp. "But I know how to get their attention. Avengers, ASSEMBLE!" Instantly, every hero turned to look at Ant-Man and Wasp.

"That's better," said Wasp. "Now, Thor, help us scatter the rest of the antidote."

Wasp sprinkled the last drops of the antidote over Mjolnir, and Thor lifted the mighty hammer into the air. Within seconds, rain started to fall.

"Noooo!" cried Scarlet Beetle, as his insect army began to shrink. "It's all over, Beetle. Thor's rainstorm is spreading the antidote," Ant-Man said.

Growing to full size, the tiny heroes grabbed the villain.
Suddenly, they heard a deep voice behind them. "Hulk SQUISH!"
And they managed to jump away just in time.

Back at Avengers Tower, the team celebrated a good end to a bad day.

"Ant-Man and Wasp, you were amazing," said Captain America. "We should have listened to you sooner."

"Oh, stop… no, keep going," joked Wasp.

Ant-Man smiled. "We're just glad that no more human-size insects are running around."

"Yeah," laughed Iron Man. "Two is more than enough!"